Wanda's Better Way

Library of Congress Cataloging-in-Publication Data

Names: Pedersen, Laura, author.
Title: Wanda's better way / by Laura Pedersen.
Description: Golden, CO : Fulcrum Publishing, [2017] | Summary: With the
   school career fair coming up young Wanda needs to decide what she wants to
   be, but as she considers the suggestions of her parents and teachers, she
   realizes that what she really wants is to invent better ways to do things.
Identifiers: LCCN 2017013528 | ISBN 9781682750148
Subjects: LCSH: Inventors--Juvenile fiction. | Inventions--Juvenile fiction.
   | Occupations--Juvenile fiction. | CYAC: Inventors--Fiction. |
   Inventions--Fiction. | Occupations--Fiction.
Classification: LCC PZ7.P34236 Wan 2017 | DDC [E]--dc23
LC record available at https://lccn.loc.gov/2017013528

Printed in South Korea.

0 9 8 7 6 5 4 3 2 1

Fulcrum Publishing
4690 Table Mountain Dr., Ste. 100
Golden, CO 80403
800-992-2908 • 303-277-1623
https://fulcrum.ipgbookstore.com

Wanda's Better Way

Written by
Laura Pedersen

Illustrated by
Penny Weber

Wanda was not in a good mood.
She was very late for her
dance class.

"Wanda, you're going to
miss class ... again!"
said Miss Watson.

"It's because this room
is always a mess.
We need cubbyholes,"
said Wanda.

"There isn't room.
We are just going to have
to practice being neat,"
said Miss Watson.

"Wanda, I know your brother loves to dance, but are you sure you really enjoy dancing? I'm wondering if you might enjoy gymnastics more," said Miss Watson.

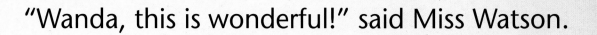

"Wanda, this is wonderful!" said Miss Watson.

8

"It's a pulley system. I saw one like it at the dry cleaner," said Wanda.

9

Wanda was starting to feel happier.
After dance class, she went to talk to her mom.

"Mom, I think I want to be a landscape designer
just like you," said Wanda.

"Great! But I thought you didn't like bugs," said Mom.

"I just won't touch them,"
said Wanda.

"Remember the plant you had in your bedroom? You forgot to water it," said Mom.
"Do you really want to spend your time gardening? If you're bored, you could walk the dog."

Wanda did not want to walk the dog.
She'd noticed something.

"Mom, did you see that
those sneaky squirrels
are eating all the birdseed?"
said Wanda.

"Why are you always making a mess?" said Ryan.

"It's not a mess," said Wanda.
"It's a project. I'm saving the birds!"

Wanda's mother was impressed with her invention.
"Wow! This is a great idea, Wanda," said Mom.

"Now the squirrels can't get
the food," said Wanda.
"But I don't think I want to be
a landscape designer anymore."

20

Wanda went inside
to see her dad.

"I want to be a chef just
like you," said Wanda.
"Will you show me how?"

"Sure!" said Dad.
"Will you separate these yolks from the egg whites?"

"This is hard," said Wanda.
"It takes so long to do."

"Sometimes things might not be easy, but they're important all the same," said Dad.

"Oops! I broke a yolk into the egg whites," said Wanda.

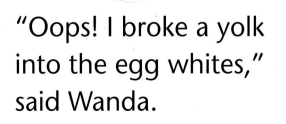

"I'm sorry, Wanda, but I have to finish this cake by tonight," said Dad. "Do you really want to spend your time baking? If you're bored, you could clean your room."

Wanda did not want to clean her room.

A week later, Wanda got to share her best idea yet.

"My dad is a chef. He spends a lot of time separating egg yolks from egg whites," said Wanda. "I think I have a better way. Can someone time us?"

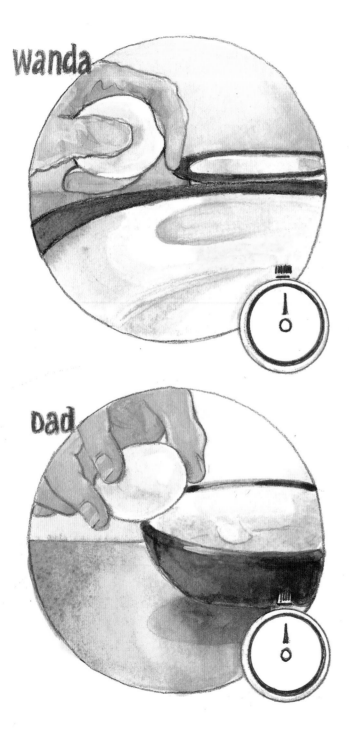

wanda

Dad

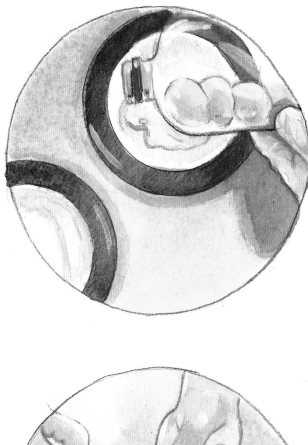

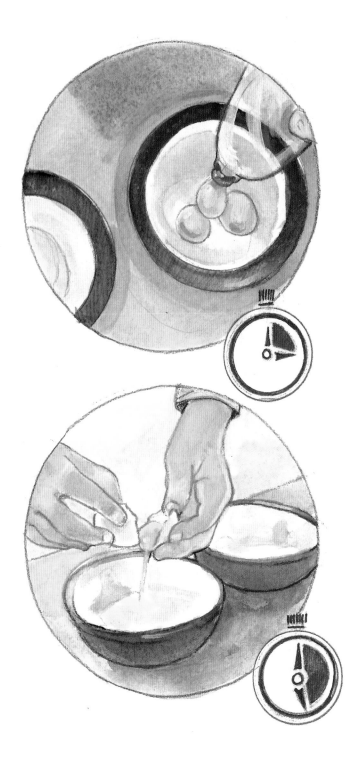

Wanda won!

"I call this 'Wanda's Better Way,'"
said Wanda.
"My way uses something called
suction. First I squeezed the air
out of the bottle. When I held it
over the egg yolks, it acted
like a vacuum and
sucked them up."

PROBLEM

MATERIALS

POTHESIS

"Good job, Wanda!"
said Dad.
"You'll be a great chef
with your better way
of doing things!"

"I don't want to be a chef.
I want to be a scientist,"
said Wanda.

"What if you have to work
with bugs?" asked Mom.

"I'll just invent something so
I don't have to touch them!"
said Wanda.

35

The Science of Solving Problems

Scientific research is all about solving problems. Wanda may not realize it, but as she invents, she is following the same *scientific method* that a scientist would to solve a problem in a laboratory.

You can find your own better way by following these steps:

1. **Observe.** Do you see a problem?
2. **Plan.** What are your goals?

3. **Brainstorm.** There might be many right answers. Think of as many as you can!
4. **Predict.** Make the best guess (hypothesis) you can about what you think your idea will do.
5. **Try.** Test your experiment. Build your invention. Follow your plan.
6. **Conclude.** Did your idea solve the problem?

The last step is very important. Many times, you won't know if you have solved a problem until after you've tried all of these steps. If your idea did *not* solve the problem:

7. **Learn.** What did you learn when you tried your idea?
8. **Try again.** Take what you've learned, and **follow the steps again**!

About the Author

Laura Pedersen is an author and playwright. A former *New York Times* columnist, Laura has written more than a dozen books for adults and children, including *Unplugged: Ella Gets Her Family Back*, and *Ava's Adventure*. *Unplugged* won a Mom's Choice Gold Award, a Moonbeam Children's Book Bronze Award for best picture book, and a Skipping Stones Honor Award.

About the Illustrator

Penny Weber works as a muralist, greeting card artist, and most recently as an illustrator for the children's market. Her work can be found in many books for children, as well as educational projects, including *Unplugged: Ella Gets Her Family Back*, *Chris P. Bacon: My Life So Far...*, and *Ava's Adventure*. Penny has a husband, three children, and a very large cat.